A Note to Parents and Teachers

DK READERS is a compelling programme for beginning readers, designed in conjunction with leading literacy experts, including Maureen Fernandes, B.Ed (Hons). Maureen has spent many years teaching literacy, both in the classroom and as a consultant in schools.

Beautiful illustrations and superb full-colour photographs combine with engaging, easy-to-read stories to offer a fresh approach to each subject in the series. Each DK READER is guaranteed to capture a child's interest while developing his or her reading skills, general knowledge, and love of reading.

The five levels of DK READERS are aimed at different reading abilities, enabling you to choose the books that are exactly right for your child:

Pre-level 1: Learning to read
Level 1: Beginning to read
Level 2: Beginning to read alone
Level 3: Reading alone
Level 4: Proficient readers

The "normal" age at which a child begins to read can be anywhere from three to eight years old. Adult participation through the lower levels is very helpful for providing encouragement, discussing storylines, and sounding out unfamiliar words.

No matter which level you select, you can be sure that you are helping your child learn to read, then read to learn!

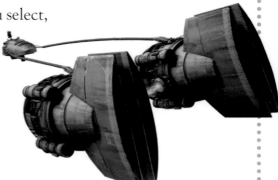

For Dorling Kindersley
Project Editor Laura Gilbert
Designer Jon Hall
Senior Slipcase Designer Mark Penfound
Senior DTP Designer Kavita Varma
Producer David Appleyard
Managing Editor Sadie Smith
Managing Art Editor Ron Stobbart
Creative Manager Sarah Harland
Art Director Lisa Lanzarini
Publisher Julie Ferris
Publishing Director Simon Beecroft

Reading Consultant Maureen Fernandes

For Lucasfilm
Executive Editor J. W. Rinzler
Art Director Troy Alders
Keeper of the Holocron Leland Chee
Director of Publishing Carol Roeder

This edition published in 2015
First published in Great Britain in 2007 by
Dorling Kindersley Limited,
80 Strand, London, WC2R 0RL

This edition produced for The Book People,
Hall Wood Avenue, Haydock, St. Helens WA11 9UL

Slipcase UI: 001–291320–Oct/15

Page design copyright © 2015 Dorling Kindersley Limited.
A Penguin Random House Company

A CIP catalogue record for this book
is available from the British Library

ISBN: 978-1-4053-2782-4

Printed in China.

www.starwars.com
www.dk.com

A WORLD OF IDEAS:
SEE ALL THERE IS TO KNOW

DK READERS

BEGINNING 1 TO READ

READY, SET, PODRACE!

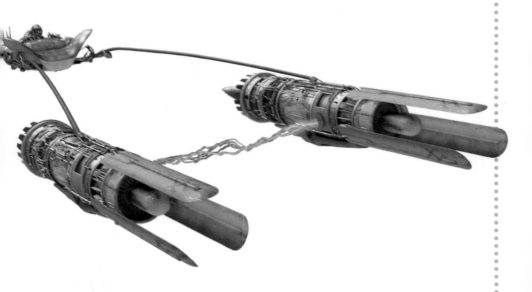

Do you like fast races?

Would you like to see
the fastest race ever?

A Podrace is the fastest race
you will ever see!

In a Podrace, each pilot flies
a machine called a Podracer.

Podracers fly just above
the ground.

Podracers fly very fast!

Podracer

Podracer pilots sit
in a seat called
a cockpit.

Cockpit

All the driving controls
are in front of them.

The pilots have to move
the controls very quickly
when they are racing.

Do you think you could fly
a Podracer?

This desert racetrack has lots of twists and turns.
Some of these twists and turns are very dangerous.

The pilot who
reaches the end
of the race first
is the winner.

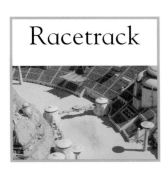

Racetrack

Many people come to watch
the Podraces.
The people shout and cheer.

They are excited to see the race.
They want to find out
which racer will win.

Podracing is very dangerous.

The pilots fly along at really
fast speeds.

Some racers crash
into each other, and
some racers crash
into desert cliffs.

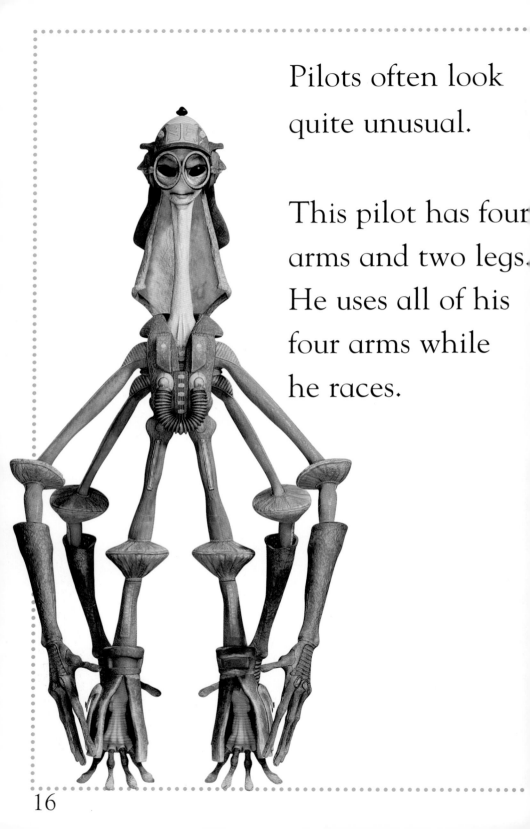

Pilots often look quite unusual.

This pilot has four arms and two legs. He uses all of his four arms while he races.

This pilot has three eyes.
His extra eye helps him
spot dangers in the race.

This pilot is wearing goggles.
They are special racing goggles.
His racing goggles
protect his eyes
from the sand in
the desert.

This pilot is nervous.
He is worried because
his Podracer is broken.
He will not finish the race.

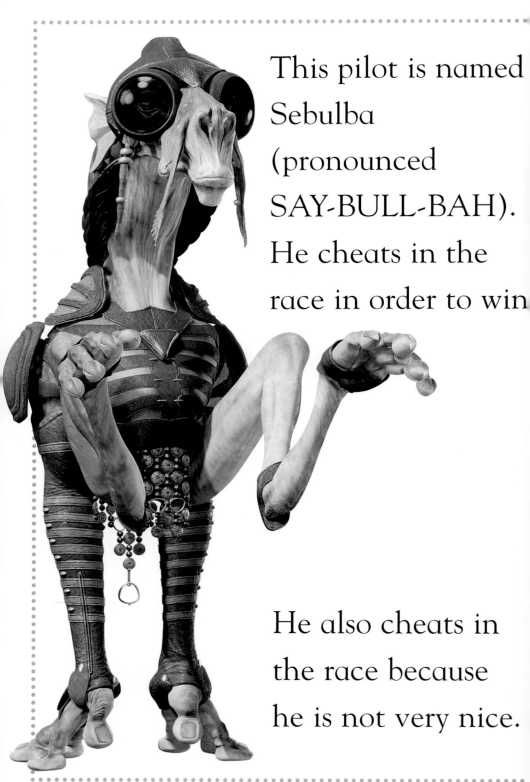

This pilot is named Sebulba (pronounced SAY-BULL-BAH). He cheats in the race in order to win

He also cheats in the race because he is not very nice.

Sebulba sometimes throws his tools at the other pilots.

He is a very dangerous racer.

Tools

To help you to read difficult words, try saying out loud the spelling in BIG TYPE. Sebulba is SAY-BULL-BAH.

Pilots prepare their machines
for the race in a big garage
called a hangar.

Robots clean
the Podracers and
repair the engines.

Each pilot makes
sure his Podracer
is ready to go!

Engines

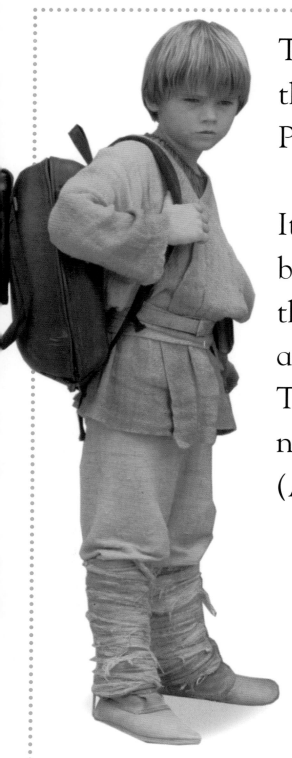

Today is one of the most exciting Podraces ever.

It is exciting because one of the racers is a young boy. The boy is named Anakin (AN-NA-KIN).

Anakin has never finished
a Podrace before.

Anakin built his Podracer all
by himself.

He is only nine years old, but he is a very good pilot.

Anakin's family and friends are going to watch him race.

The pilots are on the starting line.
Ready, steady,
Podrace!

The race is very exciting.
Sebulba does everything he can
to win.
He tries to push Anakin out
of the race.

Anakin is a better racer
than Sebulba.
Sebulba crashes!

Anakin wins the race.
Anakin's friends and family are
very happy, but Anakin is
happiest of all!

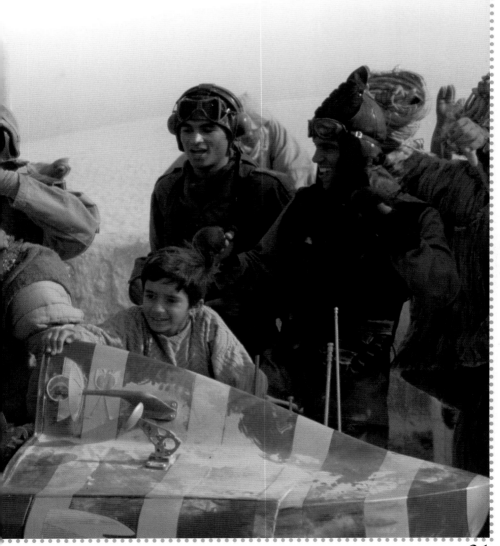

Glossary

Cockpit
a space that a pilot sits in

Engines
machines that make a vehicle move

Podracer
a vehicle that flies close to the ground

Racetrack
an oval piece of track that vehicles race on

Tools
items that are used for mechanical work